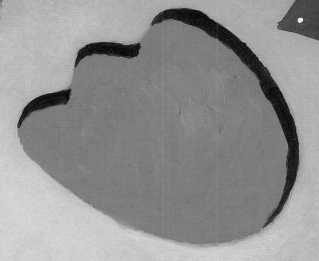
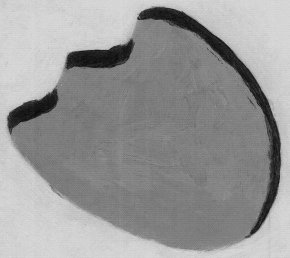

**To Mum & Joe
for their inspiration
M.M.**

First published in 2007 in Great Britain by Gullane Children's Books,
an imprint of Pinwheel Limited, Winchester House, 259-269 Old Marylebone Road, London NW1 5XJ
Text copyright © 2007 by Mark Marshall
Illustrations copyright © 2007 by Mark Marshall

This 2007 edition published by Backpack Books by arrangement with Pinwheel Ltd.

ISBN-13: 978-0-7607-9175-2
ISBN-10: 0-7607-9175-9

Printed and bound in China

1 3 5 7 9 10 8 6 4 2

Little Lion Lost!

Mark Marshall

BACK
PACK
BOOKS

Little Lion was playing in the warm afternoon sun.

He especially loved to chase frogs!

But Little Lion ran too far into the jungle,
and he soon realized he was lost and alone.
He looked around and spotted some footprints.
They could be my mom's, thought Little Lion.

And he scampered on until the footprints led him to . . .

. . . Crocodile.

"Hello, crocodile. Have you
seen my mom?" asked Little Lion.
"No, I haven't seen her," snapped crocodile,
"but I will help you look."

With a splash and a mighty
flick of his tail, crocodile was gone.
"Wait," spluttered Little Lion, "I can't swim!"

Alone again, Little Lion decided to follow a new set of footprints. *Wow, I can fit all of my paws in one of these!* he thought.

The enormous prints led him to . . .

...Elephant.

"Hello, Elephant. Have you seen
my mom?" asked Little Lion.
"No, I haven't seen her," she trumpeted,
"but I will help you look."

The ground shook as Elephant charged off.

"Wait for me!" panted Little Lion, but he couldn't keep up with Elephant's huge strides.

Alone again, he decided to
follow a new set of footprints.
This time they led him to . . .

. . . Monkey

"Hello, Monkey!" called Little Lion.
"Have you seen my mom?"
"No, I haven't seen her," he
chattered, "but I will help you look."

With a loud rustle, Monkey swung though the tree-tops and disappeared.
"Wait, Monkey," Little Lion shouted, "I don't think I can climb this tree!"

Alone again, Little Lion wished he could find his mom's footprints.

Crocodile's were **webbed**.

Elephant's were just **ENORMOUS**.

And Monkey's were far too **long and thin!**

Where can she be?

"I think it's time to go home,"
Said a familiar voice.
Little Lion spun around to see . . .

...Mommy!

"I've been looking everywhere for you,"
he purred, "how did you find me?"
"Well, that's simple," she said,
"I followed *your* footprints!"

Little Lion sat on his mom's back and together they followed their footprints all the way home.